THE SWAN MAIDEN

For Kelli Lyn and Nicole
E.G.

To my wife, Suzanne,
and the transformative powers of Love.
R.S.

Library of Congress Cataloging-in-Publication Data
Pyle, Howard, 1853–1911.
The Swan Maiden / by Howard Pyle ; selected and with an afterword
by Ellin Greene ; illustrated by Robert Sauber. — 1st ed.
p.   cm.
Summary: The king's youngest son releases the Swan Maiden from
servitude under the witch with three eyes.
ISBN 0-8234-1088-9
[1. Fairy tales.]   I. Greene, Ellin.   II. Sauber, Rob,
ill.   III. Title.
PZ8.P991Sw   1994   93-34605   CIP   AC
[E]—dc20

THE SWAN MAIDEN

by Howard Pyle

afterword by Ellin Greene

illustrated by Robert Sauber

Holiday House/New York

Once there was a king who had a pear tree which bore four-and-twenty golden pears. Every day he went into the garden and counted them to see that none were missing. But one morning he found that a pear had been taken during the night, and thereat he was troubled, for the pear tree was as dear to him as the apple of his eye.

Now the king had three sons, so he called the eldest prince to him and said, "If you will watch my pear tree tonight and catch the thief who stole the pear, you shall have half of my kingdom now, and the whole of it when I am gone."

You can guess how this pleased the prince. Oh, yes, he would watch the pear tree, and if the thief should come again he should not get away so easily.

That night, the eldest prince sat down beside the tree, with his gun across his knees, to wait for the coming of the thief. He waited and waited, and still he saw not so much as a thread or a hair. But about midnight there came the prettiest music that his ears had ever heard, and before he knew what he was about he was asleep and snoring until the little leaves shook upon the tree.

When morning came and the prince awoke, another pear was gone, and he could tell no more about it than the man in the moon.

The next night the second son set out to watch the pear tree, but he fared no better than the first. About midnight he heard the music, and in a little while he was snoring until the stones rattled. When morning came another pear was gone, and he could tell no more about it than his brother.

The third night it was the turn of the youngest prince. He was more clever than his brothers for he stuffed his ears full of wax so that when the music came he heard none of it and stayed wide awake. When midnight passed and the music had ended, he took the wax out of his ears so that he might listen for the coming of the thief. Presently, there was a loud clapping and rattling, and a white swan flew overhead and lit in the pear tree above him. It began pecking at one of the pears. The prince raised his gun to shoot at it, but, when he looked along the barrel of the gun, it was not a swan that he saw, but the prettiest maiden that he had ever looked upon.

"Don't shoot me, king's son! Don't shoot me!" she cried.

But the prince had no thought of shooting her for he had never seen anyone so beautiful in all of his days. "Very well," he said, "I will not shoot, but, if I spare your life, will you promise to be my sweetheart and to marry me?"

"That may be as may be," said the Swan Maiden, "for I serve the witch with three eyes. She lives on the glass hill that lies beyond the seven high mountains, the seven deep valleys, and the seven wide rivers. Are you man enough to go that far?"

"Yes," said the prince, "I am man enough for that and more."

"That is good," said the Swan Maiden, and thereupon she jumped down from the pear tree to the earth. Then she became a swan again and bade the king's son to mount upon her back at the roots of her wings. When he had done as she had told him, she sprang into the air and flew away, bearing him with her.

On flew the swan, and on and on, until, by and by, she said, "What do you see, king's son?"

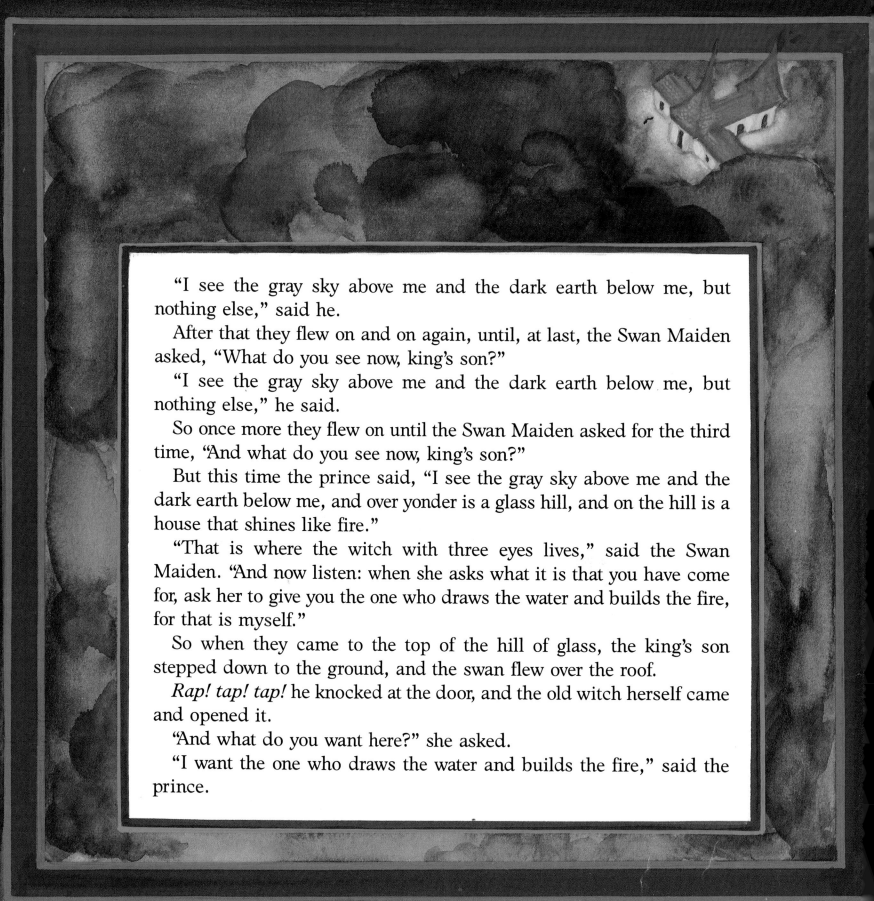

"I see the gray sky above me and the dark earth below me, but nothing else," said he.

After that they flew on and on again, until, at last, the Swan Maiden asked, "What do you see now, king's son?"

"I see the gray sky above me and the dark earth below me, but nothing else," he said.

So once more they flew on until the Swan Maiden asked for the third time, "And what do you see now, king's son?"

But this time the prince said, "I see the gray sky above me and the dark earth below me, and over yonder is a glass hill, and on the hill is a house that shines like fire."

"That is where the witch with three eyes lives," said the Swan Maiden. "And now listen: when she asks what it is that you have come for, ask her to give you the one who draws the water and builds the fire, for that is myself."

So when they came to the top of the hill of glass, the king's son stepped down to the ground, and the swan flew over the roof.

Rap! tap! tap! he knocked at the door, and the old witch herself came and opened it.

"And what do you want here?" she asked.

"I want the one who draws the water and builds the fire," said the prince.

At this the old witch scowled until her eyebrows met.

"Very well," she said, "you shall have what you want if you can clean my stables tomorrow between the rise and the set of the sun. But I tell you plainly, if you fail in the doing, you shall be torn to pieces, body and bones."

But the prince was not to be scared away with empty words. So the next morning the old witch came and took him to the stables where he was to do his task. There stood more than a hundred cattle, and the stable had not been cleaned in ten long years!

"There is your work," said the old witch, and left him.

Well, the king's son set to work with fork and broom and might and main, but he might as well have tried to bail out the great ocean with a bucket.

At noon, who should come to the stable but the Swan Maiden.

"When one is tired, one should rest awhile," she said. "Come and lay your head in my lap."

The prince was glad enough to do as she said, for nothing was to be gained by working at that task. So he laid his head in her lap, and she combed his hair with a golden comb until he fell fast asleep.

When the prince awoke the Swan Maiden was gone, the sun was setting, and the stable was as clean as a plate. Presently, he heard the old witch coming, so up he jumped and began clearing away a straw here and a speck there, just as though he were finishing the work.

"You never did this by yourself!" said the old witch, and her brows grew as black as a thunderstorm.

"That may be so, and that may not be so," said the king's son, "but you lent no hand to help. So now may I have the one who builds the fire and draws the water?"

At this the old witch shook her head. "No, there is more to be done before you can have what you ask for. If you can thatch the roof of my stable with bird feathers, no two of which shall be of the same color, and can do it between the rise and the set of the sun tomorrow, then you may have your sweetheart. But if you fail, your bones shall be ground as fine as malt in the mill."

Very well, that suited the king's son well enough. So at sunrise he arose and went into the fields with his gun. But if there were birds to be shot, it was few of them that he saw, and by noon he had but two, and they were both of the same color. Then who should come but the Swan Maiden.

"One should not tramp and tramp all day with never a bit of rest," said she. "Come and lay your head in my lap for a while."

The prince did as she bade him, and once again she combed his hair with a golden comb until he fell asleep. When he awoke the sun was setting, and his work was done. He heard the old witch coming, so up he jumped to the roof of the stable and began laying a feather here and a feather there, for all the world as though he were just finishing his task.

"You never did that work alone," said the old witch.

"That may be so, and that may not be so," said the prince. "All the same, it was none of your doing. So now may I have the one who draws the water and builds the fire?"

But the witch shook her head. "No, there is still another task to do before that. Over yonder is a fir tree. On that tree is a crow's nest, and in the nest are three eggs. If you can rob that nest tomorrow between the rising and the setting of the sun, neither breaking nor leaving a single egg, you shall have that for which you ask."

Very well, that suited the prince. The next morning at the rising of the sun he started off to find the fir tree, and there was no trouble in the finding I can tell you, for it was more than a hundred feet high, and as smooth as glass from root to tip. As for climbing it, he might as well have tried to climb a moonbeam, for in spite of all his trying he did nothing but slip and slip. By and by came the Swan Maiden as she had come before.

"Do you climb the fir tree?" said she.

"None too well," said he.

"Then I may help you in a hard task," said she.

She let down the braids of her golden hair so that it hung down all about her and upon the ground, and then she began singing to the wind. She sang and sang, and by and by the wind began to blow, and, catching up the maiden's hair, carried it to the top of the fir tree, and there tied it to the branches. Then the prince climbed the hair and so reached the nest. There were the three eggs. He gathered them and then came down as he had gone up. After that the wind came again and loosed the maiden's hair from the branches, and she bound it up as it was before.

"Now, listen," she said to the prince, "when the old witch asks you for the three crow's eggs, tell her they belong to the one who gathered them. She will not be able to take them from you, and they are worth something, I can tell you."

At sunset the old witch came hobbling along, and there sat the prince at the foot of the fir tree.

"Have you gathered the crow's eggs?" she asked.

"Yes," said the prince, "here they are in my handkerchief. And now may I have the one who draws the water and builds the fire?"

"Yes," said the old witch, "you may have her, only give me my crow's eggs."

"No," said the prince, "the crow's eggs are none of yours for they belong to him who gathered them."

When the old witch found she was not to get the crow's eggs in that way, she tried another, and began using words as sweet as honey. Come, come, there should be no hard feeling between them. The prince had served her faithfully, and before he went home with what he had come for he should have a good supper, for it is ill to travel on an empty stomach.

So she brought the prince into the house, and then she left him while she went to put the pot on the fire, and to sharpen the bread knife on the stone doorstep.

While the prince sat waiting for the witch, there came a tap at the door, and who should it be but the Swan Maiden.

"Come," she said, "and bring the three eggs with you, for the knife that the old witch is sharpening is for you, and so is the great pot on the fire, for she means to pick your bones in the morning."

She led the prince down into the kitchen. There they made a figure out of honey and barley meal, so that it was all soft and sticky. Then the Swan Maiden dressed the figure in her own clothes and set it in the chimney corner by the fire.

After that was done, she became a swan again, and, taking the prince upon her back, she flew away, over hill and over dale.

As for the old witch, she sat on the stone doorstep, sharpening her knife. By and by she came in, but, look as she might, there was no prince to be found.

Then if anybody was ever in a rage it was the old witch. Off she went, storming and fuming, until she came to the kitchen. There sat the woman of honey and barley meal beside the fire, dressed in the Swan Maiden's clothes, and the old woman thought it was the girl herself. "Where is your sweetheart?" she asked. But to this the woman of honey and barley meal answered not a word.

"How now! Are you dumb?" cried the old witch. "I will see whether I cannot bring speech to your lips." She raised her hand—*slap!*—she struck, and so hard was the blow that her hand stuck fast to the honey and barley meal. "What!" she cried, "will you hold me?"—*slap!*—she struck with the other hand, and it too stuck fast. So there she was, and, for all I know, she is sticking to the woman of honey and barley meal to this day.

As for the Swan Maiden and the prince, they flew over the seven high mountains, the seven deep valleys, and the seven wide rivers, until they came near to the prince's home again. The Swan Maiden lit in a great wide field, and there she told the prince to break open the crow's eggs. When he broke open the first egg, what should he find but the most beautiful little castle all of pure gold and silver. He set the castle on the ground, and it grew and grew and grew until it covered as much ground as seven large barns. When he broke open the second egg, out of it came such great herds of cows and sheep that they covered the meadow far and near. And when he broke open the third egg, out of it came more than a hundred servants dressed in silver and gold.

That morning, when the king looked out of his bedroom window, there stood the splendid castle of silver and gold. Then he called all of his people together, and they rode over to see what it meant. On the way they passed such herds of fat sheep and cattle that the king had never seen the like in all of his days. When he came to the fine castle, two rows of servants dressed in silver and gold uniforms saluted him, and when he came to the door of the castle, there stood his youngest son waiting to greet him. Then there was joy and rejoicing, you may be sure! Only the two elder brothers looked down in the mouth, for since their young brother had found the thief who stole the golden pears, their father's kingdom was not for them. But the prince soon set their minds at rest on that score for he had enough and more than enough of his own.

After that, the prince and the Swan Maiden were married, and a grand wedding it was, with music of fiddles and kettledrums, and plenty to eat and to drink. I, too, was there, but all that I came away with was this story.

And that is all.

AFTERWORD

With the publication of *The Merry Adventures of Robin Hood of Great Renown in Nottinghamshire* in 1883, Howard Pyle (1853–1911) established himself as "one of America's foremost writers and illustrators for children." Pyle's talents for writing and illustrating were inseparable. His writing is full of word-pictures; his drawings are alive with movement, animated with accurate detail.

In an autobiographical sketch, "When I Was a Little Boy," published in *The Woman's Home Companion* (April 1912), Pyle noted that his mother read aloud fairy tales of the Brothers Grimm "til he knew them almost by heart." It was natural that he turned to the folktale for inspiration when he began writing his own fairy tales. His command of the form of the folktale is what makes his stories so tellable. Pyle used the rhythm and repetition of the folktale, its themes and motifs, and what folklorists call the framing device. In the preface to his collection, *The Wonder Clock* (Harper, 1888), from which "The Swan Maiden" is taken, Pyle tells of finding an old clock in Time's garret which, whenever it struck the hour, brought forth the "drollest little puppet-figures" who engaged in a dance. Pyle wrote, and illustrated in pen and ink, a story for each hour of the day.

In my retelling I have used a light hand, shortening the tale somewhat for oral presentation, but retaining Pyle's picturesque phrases. Pyle's tone is conversational, his pace brisk. In his tales, one finds kindly humor, plenty of action, and vigorous prose. His tales are a rich source for the storyteller.

Howard Pyle was regarded as one of the best teachers of illustration in America. Among his students can be counted Maxfield Parrish, N.C. Wyeth, and Jessie Wilcox Smith. Pyle believed that creative imagination was the quality most needed by an illustrator. No matter how technically excellent, it was not enough to depict the happenings in the text. The artist must draw upon his imagination to bring to life the inner meaning and significance of the story. Pyle's rigorous standards, his emphasis on the importance of the imagination, and his encouragement of individual expression continue to challenge and inspire children's book illustrators today.

—Ellin Greene